by Peggy Perry Anderson

ISBN 978-1-7333462-8-3 (hard cover)

ISBN 978-1-7333462-7-6 (paperback)

Doodle and Peck Publishing

413 Cedarburg Ct

Yukon, Oklahoma 73099

(405) 354-7422

www.doodleandpeck.com

Page layout and design by Brandon Anderson

Library of Congress Control Number: 2020932482

Dedicated to all my
cat-loving cousins. And, of course, my grandchildren,
Jacob, Céo, Luke, Leira
and Ayzen.

Peggy Perry Anderson

Simple activities designed to help parents and/or caregivers participate in, and support, a child's literacy skills and educational goals:

- **Easiest: Read the story together then sing the alphabet song. Next, place alphabet cards* in alphabetical order, using the song for hints.**
- **More Difficult: Find these words* in the book and talk about their meaning--**cat, fur, kitten, paws, nose, eye, mouth, tail
- **Challenging: Assist your child in researching "cat" on your computer or at the library. Next, have them list three or more facts* about cats.**

*For free, printable resources, visit www.doodleandpeck.com, click on the Linking to Literacy tab.

Orange, yellow, black or white,
Asleep by day, awake at night.

Fluffy, furry, velvety, bare. . .
They can have all kinds of hair.

Striped, solid, dotted, too,
Catching mice is what they do.

Limp as jello or bouncy as springs,
They like to hide inside of things.

I'm sure by now you must know that
We are reading about the cat.

But if you want to know them better
We must look at every letter!

Alexander the acrobat laughs at

Aa

Bb

big, bad Boris
biting a bundt cake

and Catherine crouching in her crate.

Cc

Darla hates to be dressed up.

She does not want to play.

Dd

Ee

But Evie likes to excercise with Ella everyday.

Ff
FRED LOVES FISH!
NO, these fish
are not for you!

Granny loves grandkittens.
Grandkittens love her, too.

Gg

Hh

Henry **hisses** at a **cactus** and becomes a **hairy** sight!

But Ivan seems
invisible
as he tiptoes in the
night.
Ii

JoAnna
enjoys her
jungle.
See the
June bug she has
found?
Jj

Kk

While her

kittens and a kid

are outside,

kidding around.

Lazy Lucy's
lava lamp makes
Lucy feel so glad.
Ll

But the collie won't let Molly eat the melon.

My, how sad.

Mm

Book Nook

Inside Nora's
nook,
she reads her favorite
book.

Nn

Oo

Outside Odie's bag,
an opossum plays tag.

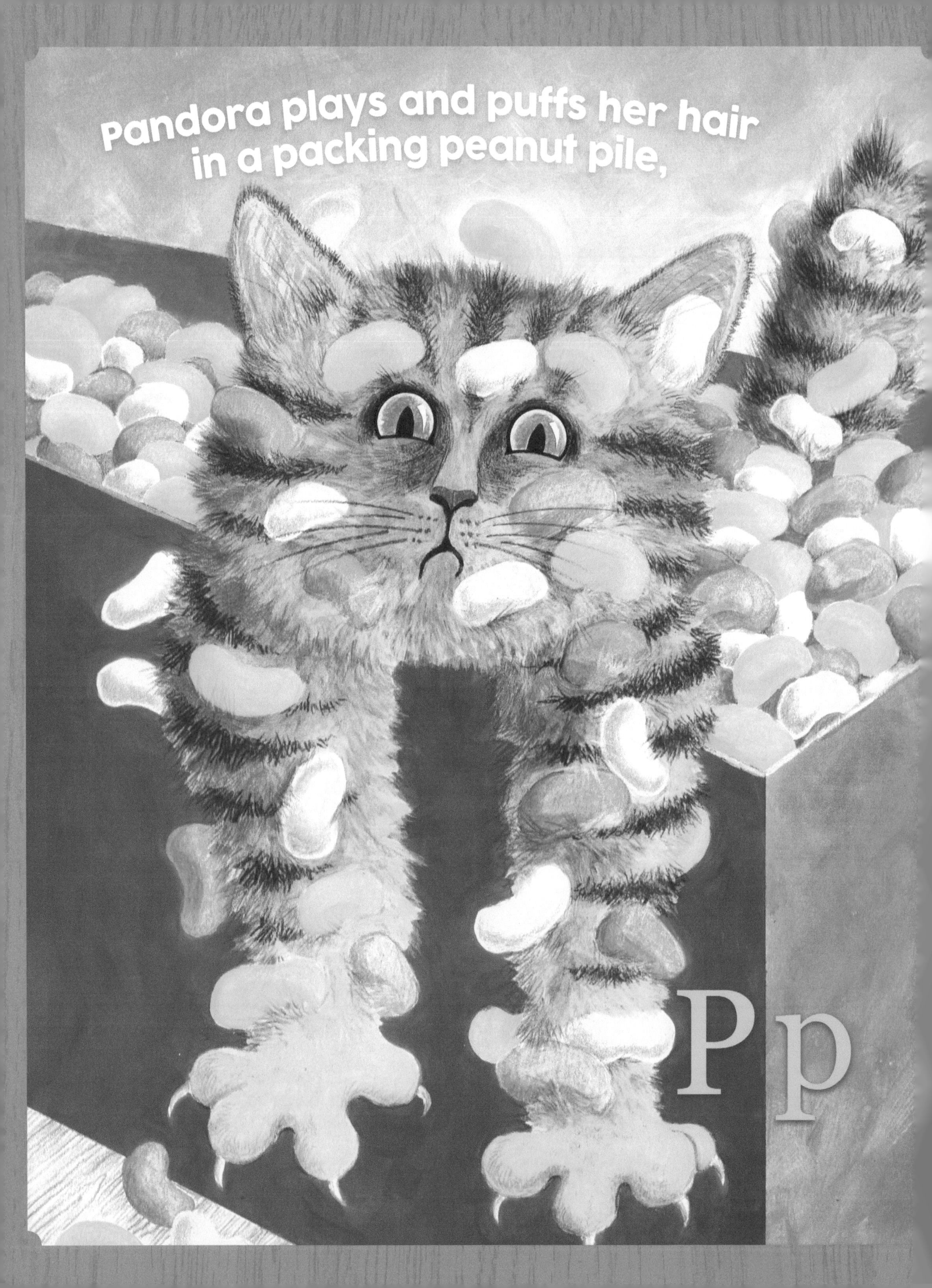
Pandora plays and puffs her hair
in a packing peanut pile,
Pp

Qq

but a catnap on a homemade
quilt is quiet Queenie's style.

Run cats! Run!
Who will win the race?
7
18
Rr
5
4

S s

Up above
in a sea of stars,
Stellar floats
in space.

Toby, Tyler, Tim and Tom
are selfish TV fellows.

Tt

On neighborhood watch, Undercover Cat is sharing his umbrella.

A vampire cat for Halloween,
Victor's fangs are scary!

Ww

Wilma watches snowflakes fall in the cold of January.

Xx
Lexi found the missing ball with her x-ray eyes.

"Yahoo!"
yelled Yancy
the
cowboy cat.
"What a
big surprise!"
Yy

Zz

This zippy cat is riding on the merry-go-round again. Zebra likes his furry friend who zooms around with him.

Now you've read this book with me

All about cats, A through Z!

Playful, gentle, happy, sad,

Curious, fearful, grumpy, mad...

I think you will not make a fuss

When I say cats are quite like us!

Meet Author and Illustrator

Peggy Anderson

With a BFA from Tulsa University, **Peggy Perry Anderson** has been a graphic artist as well as an art teacher. While illustrating picture books for other authors, Anderson wrote and illustrated 10 books published by Houghton Mifflin Harcourt, such as, *We Go in a Circle* and *To the Tub. Chuck's Truck* was a finalist for the Oklahoma Book Award.

Peggy Anderson received the Governor's Award of Excellence for her work in children's literature. You may view Anderson's work at **www.peggyperryanderson.com**.